Sascha Martin's Rocket-Ship

Written by John Arthur Nichol
Illustrated by Manuela Pentangelo

www.johnarthurnicholauthor.com

Cover photo of Sam Ridgway and her rocket by Richard Termini

ISBN-13: 978-0-9954183-0-1

For my three children,
Peter, Jeffrey and David,
and for
my granddaughter,
Charlotte

Rocketry is a nail-biting, breath-holding experience

Photo by Richard Termini

I love books, I love kids and I love rockets! So I was thrilled to see all three combined in John Arthur Nichol's new Sascha Martin series of adventures for children.

Sascha Martin's Rocket Ship is first in the series and will launch its readers into an adventure that should fan the flames of curiosity for science in almost any girl or boy. The story is 'poetry in motion' for rocket ships! Manuela Pentangelo has visually interpreted John's verse with all the best icons from rocketry and science in the gorgeous illustrations.

I had no idea that my own experience with home-made rockets would make me Australia's first woman to officially fly a Level 3 High-Power rocket and then ignite my desire to complete a science degree at university! So, I encourage all parents to give the hobby a go with their kids after reading this book – who knows the exciting places the experience may take them?

Rocketry is always a nail-biting, breath-holding experience but I cannot claim to have ever launched one accidentally! Some of our rocket-ships have had unexpected landings on rocks or in 2 metre high weeds; or the parachute has caught a thermal breeze and the rocket drifted further afield than predicted, but each flight is always unique and a learning event.

Kids and Science are our future, and rockets are humankind's most exciting invention so like Sascha, let's be bold, creative and curious. The sky's the limit.

Samantha Ridgway
Perth, WA
August 1, 2016

For my photos and true-life rocketry exploits please go to http://www.therocketwoman.com

Photo by Richard Termini

Photo by Gloria Salgado Gispert

Sascha Martin

Sascha Martin, Class 2M
and only 8 years old

Inventor

Is a genius at inventing things that won't do what they're told

Luca Blanco

Luca Blanco lives near Sascha
by The Wilderness - they're friends

And his pockets always rattle with
collected odd and ends

Mary-Alice Cooper

Mary-Alice is their neighbour
and she always needs to know
She's the centre of attention
and the star of every show

And she reckons she's a friend of theirs;
they say it isn't true
But she makes the boys include her
just by nagging till they do

Mrs. Barnum

Mrs Barnum is a clockwork teacher - organised, precise -

And her students almost like her in the moments when she's nice

Mr. Jack

Mr Jack is fond of eating,
cups of tea, and smiles a lot

And his class is pretty noisy
but he teaches when they're not

Sascha Martin's rocket-ship
was twice the teacher's height.
He brought it in for news one day
(his mum had said all right).

He left it on the table
with a note that said "Don't Touch!"
So someone pushed a button
and the rocket started such

A roaring, then went silent,
then it gave a mighty ...

And Sascha grabbed the rocket
as the rocket left the room

It flew across the playground
with a piercing kind of wail
(That was Sascha hanging screaming
from the rocket's burning tail).

Children tumbled from their classrooms
looking skyward with concern
Seeming not to hear their teachers
who insisted they return.

Sascha rocketed above them
like a spectre (pale with fright)
But they laughed and yelled and giggled,
(not bethinking of his plight)

Till the rocket dived among them
and accelerated fast
On a beeline for the room
where Mrs Barnum stood aghast.

Through the window went the rocket

Through the room

and out the door

Then it looped a loop and headed
for the Tuck-Shop in the Hall

Where the mums and dads were busy
with the pies for lunch that day …
Till the rocket scooped the oven up
and carried it away

Dropping pies and bits of birthday cake
on parent volunteers
Then erupting through the roof
(the children greeted it with cheers)

But the cheering stopped when
Sascha's rocket
headed for the ground
And the children ran for cover.
Sascha's eyes were big and round

And he wasn't very happy
(you could tell, the way he squealed)
Then the rocket raised its head and
sped towards the lower field

Where the children on the oval
playing volleyball looked round
And they scattered as the rocket passed them
just above the ground.

As they watched the missile spin about
to make a second pass,
They heard Sascha screaming, "Save me!"
and his bottom scraped the grass.

When he gathered speed and headed for
the children once again,
Mr Jack and Mrs Barnum
made an urgent plan and then ...

Held the net strung out between them
pulling really, really tight,
And they braced themselves to catch and hold
the rocket in its flight.

Then the rocket hit the net,
the net extended, more and more,
The rocket started slowing down,
it coughed, and gave a roar,

But then it found a second wind
and tore the net away,
And with it came the teachers
who had tried to make it stay.

The rocket carried Sascha
and the oven and the net,
Mr Jack and Mrs Barnum
(who were voicing their regret)

In a spiral and a wiggle
and a circle and a roar

Then it tilted fully
vertical
and up and up it tore.

As the children watched in wonder,
as the lunchtime hooter blew,
Sascha's rocket simply vanished
in the sky's enormous blue.

Well lunchtime passed in wondering,
with all the faces raised -
all documenting everything
as ever up they gazed

Till a squeaky little voice rang out,
a finger pointed high,
And sure enough a speck of light
was shining in the sky.

The speck grew ever larger as
the children watched in awe;
The rocket coming down again
looked bigger than before,

Which they couldn't understand
till one among them gave a hoot,
For the rocket was attached to
an enormous ...

parachute

Mrs Barnum touched down first
and Mr Jack behind her fell.
The net and then the oven
and the rocket came as well,

Then Sascha, then the parachute
that settled over all …
Then a deluge of the other flying
things began to fall

When it stopped, the children screamed
and they were wild like buccaneers
As they tore away the parachute
to find the rocketeers.

Mrs B was blown away, bereft,
befuddled and bemused
Mr J was jibber-jabbering,
and jumpy and confused.

Only Sascha had a greeting
and a shaky kind of smile,
But he said he mightn't build
another rocket for a while.

At the school they spoke of nothing
but The Incident for days,
Every classroom conversation,
every drawing, every phrase

Had a flashing silver missile,
screaming teachers and a net;

Sascha Martin was a hero!
It took ages to forget.

Now the school is back to normal -
only little things have changed;
The pies are shaped like rocket-ships,
the oven's been exchanged,

They had to put a skylight in the
ceiling of the hall,
And the staff-room has a window
where there used to be a wall.

And of course, a certain day each week
just crackles with suspense,
With the children looking eager
and the teachers looking tense …

It's the day when Mr Jack and
Mrs Barnum hide away;
They'll be doing that this morning
cause it's Sascha's News today.

Keep an eye out for these upcoming titles:

Sascha Martin's Time Machine

Sascha Martin's Superball

Sascha Martin's Zombie Dust

Sascha Martin's Visitor

Sascha Martin's Aliens

Sascha Martin's Dinosaurs

Sascha Martin's Gobbly Goo

Sascha Martin's Christmas Witch

Visit www.johnarthurnicholauthor.com
for updates and news

https://www.facebook.com/SaschaMartinsAdventures/
http://saschamartinadventures.jimdo.com/

CPSIA information can be obtained
at www.ICGtesting.com
Printed in the USA
BVHW020922220419
546167BV00027B/2078/P

9 780995 418301